C000009395

# Whispers to a Crow

Tristan Gray

Copyright © 2020 Tristan Gray

All rights reserved.

ISBN: 9-798675-960170

# ACKNOWLEDGMENTS

First and foremost, my thanks go to my partner Jude Telford who has supported me crafting this tale even whilst I guarded its contents away until I was certain it deserved being read. Thank you for your endless encouragement and patience. Everything is easier knowing you are with me every step of the way.

To my Mum and Dad, who inspired my creativity from my very earliest memories, without which I would never have set hands to a keyboard to begin with. To my brother, Callum, who I forged so many of those memories with.

Thank you to Gillian Hamnett from Dark Sky Pages for going above and beyond with her work on the Scots dialogue editing. She helped shape the words of Oeric, Ingram, and Simon to give them, and the Three Willows, the foundation they needed to build this story from.

Thank you to Margaret Kingsbury, editor for Salt & Sage Books, for her work on the developmental edit that gave this story its upgrade it needed to become my first published piece of work. Her guidance was exactly the support I needed to complete these forty-odd pages. To Erin Olds, as well, for keeping on top of my messy emails and keeping the two of us in touch.

To my friends Matt, Vinn, John, Ben, and Joy, thank you for your help with the final polishes and putting up with my seemingly endless mentions of the existence of drafts you never actually were able to see. I hope the wait was worth it!

# WHISPERS TO A CROW

A lonely light shone in the darkness, a single candle-lit lantern swinging from the tavern's door through the fog. A single beaten path led to its door, far from the well-travelled road.

This was no place for travellers. There was no stable to shelter her steed, nor a sign to announce some alliterative name that waifs would remember and pass on to their fellows in other taverns along the way.

But this was the place. Too far for any but the desperate to travel to, where only an empty purse could make the journey worthwhile.

She dismounted and knotted Dìleas' reins about the sturdiest post of the dilapidated fence. With cloak pulled close against the bite of the night's wind, she walked to the door and gave it a push.

The wood lurched free of her palm to slam open, the wind coursing through to sweep up the curses and grumbles of nearby patrons.

She hauled the door shut with squeals of complaints from its hinges, but it had been closed barely a moment before the eyes of the room had moved on. To cards, to coins, to mead and beer. Anything but the black-clad newcomer who'd brought in the autumn chill.

A pall had fallen upon this place. No laughter between

comrades in from the fields. No brazen bets and sordid tales ringing between the rafters. Two dozen men in silence bode well for no one.

There was one who caught her attention, however. A coin turned over in one palm, the other's fingers drumming away the time. Someone waiting for something in a room of many waiting for nothing.

His eyes were on her when she sat across from him, the coin abruptly halting its journey across his knuckles. His eyes quickly ran along her blades, the longsword across her back and the hilts of knives strapped to her side.

The few about him muttered and whispered to one another as they fixed eyes upon her, one made the sign of their god across his chest, but the man before her shushed them. "Enough, it's ma coin, it's ma business whit ah dae wi' it," he snapped to them. "Youse do wi' yours how ye choose."

"The Craw?" he said to her, turning and looking her up and down with a barely concealed sneer. "Ye dinnae look like whit ah expected frae a Craw."

"What did you expect?" Her Àrdish was learned from old books rather than the tongue of the north, but she spoke it well enough.

He shrugged. "Ah dinnae ken. Big black eyes, mebbe some feathers pokin' oot frae yer tunic. A necklace o' beaked skulls aboot yer neck? No just a wee lass wi' eerie eyes, that's fir sure."

It wasn't exactly the cry for help she had been expecting, but nor did it drip with the open contempt she was so used to in the south.

"You called for a Crow and you promised some coin. I'm afraid you'll be waiting for another to sweep in on feathered wings," she said, her hands joined at the thumb in a weak imitation. "So how about you explain to this Crow what kind of creature you have at hand, now?" The words came with a smile dimpling her cheek.

The smile was not reciprocated. The contempt was there,

sure enough, clear on the faces of the men turning their backs about him.

"No yin but mony, Craw. Ye can hear them in the nicht, the bayin' o' a score o' hounds, a monster sent by the deevil ready tae snatch us awa'." His eyes dropped now; it was easier to speak to a stranger if you pretended it was something else. The hand not preoccupied with the coin was now held tight around the wooden pendant hanging from his neck, his knuckles white.

He continued, "It aw stertit wi' the eve o' summer. It was just yin, first. Ye ken how it goes, Craw. A wee yin falls intae some pairt they cannae be found, a parent hushes up a mishap, tries tae hinder gossip o' an ailing that could spread. But then anither, an' anither."

"Ye lose a few yins. Happens, no township goes withoot a few younglings lost wi' the changing o' the seasons. But no a dozen. No in yin summer wi' no track or trail o' the lost."

She felt a chill then, the weight that hung over the tavern starting to manifest with every detail spoken. There were no smiles now.

His hands were wrapped over one another now, sequestering the coin away from her gaze. There was a mark on one finger, a divot where the flesh had been compressed by a band wrapped around it for many years. He had lost someone too, this foreman, though it will have been many winters ago.

"Oor priest telt us no tae fret, that a gid harvest would come if we prayed and cleansed oorselves, that some o' us had sinned and The Lord Most High had led the pure awa'."

"More went missin'. Some o' us stopped listenin' in time, Lord save their souls. They accused the faither o' lyin' tae them, something tae dae wi' his servant."

His words came fiercer now, the words spat forth, "a veil o' sorrow fell on the Willows. Too mony gone, too mony angry. He left us, he stopped answerin' the howls o' grief at his door, the bastart! He aye promised us the harvest, but the harvest fell soor. The rot claimed it, it claimed some o' ma men, tae. We left him in his place o' faith surrounded by nocht but death."

"This isn't your town?" she said, hands flat between them.

"It's naebody's toon. Just a place between places."

*A place between places for a Crow with no place to go. It has a poetry to it,* she thought.

"You mentioned there were accusations about the priest's servant," she said, hands open. "Why? Seems an unlikely target for the grief of lost children."

The response came with a sneer. "She wisnae richt, that yin. Arrivin' withoot warnin' wi' the winter snaws, nae yin o' us. She didnae speak wi' us, didnae share oor food or in oor services. She seemed no tae pray or tak the bread, strange for a priest's servant, ye ken? She wisnae richt, wisnae o' the faith. No richt for a priest to keep such company."

"You believe he was breaking his vows?"

"Ah believe he'd been led astray. Ah cast nae judgement on a servant o' the Lord."

He might believe that, even if the gods saw through it..

One of his companions tapped him on the shoulder and leaned in to whisper into his ear. She threaded her fingers together on the table. This kind of thing wasn't new to her. Especially down here in the lowlands, a town would deliberate when help didn't come from a lord or temple and settle on hiring a Crow. But they didn't want to do it, it was never their first resort, and the moment the topic came to discussing whatever magics plagued them, real or imagined, some had second thoughts.

Every single time they began this frantic aggressive whispering to one another, discussing the wisdom of having 'one of them' about when they had enough trouble already. She caught the foreman's name, Oeric, and some disagreement over pointing a Crow towards a temple.

Fiadh wished they'd have had this discussion over and done with before she sat just across from them.

The second farmer glanced up to see her eyes still on them and snapped, "whit's that Craw? Huv ye got the hearin' o' an owl and aw?"

"Well, no, but you are barely two yards from my head, speak your words to me directly. If you do not trust me to get the job done, then do not put out a sign for a Crow. Give me your task, or tell me to go, your choice. But if I'm staying, I'm going to need to know what happened to your priest."

She waited as they flitted their eyes back and forth from her to one another, but their foreman did not leave the silence long before speaking.

"Still boarded up in the temple, for aw ah ken. Surroonded by nocht but the rot. Me and ma lads are here ti' the months' end. The Ealdorman at Dun Caraich hasnae deigned tae bless us wi' his ain, so we're left tae pit notice oot fir a Craw. Pray that this is ower before Seanadh twa morrows hence, before the slaugh taks whit's left frae us."

"Slaugh?" The restless dead who legends told would flock from the west in the winter months to steal away those who might leave a path for them open. The Seanadh was a festival of the old gods meant to keep them at bay; it seems the priest wasn't particularly good at the job he was appointed for.

The man grumbled into his drink, "aye, Ah'm a follower o' the Lord, it's true, but ye don't go messin' wi' auld powers on their festival days. It's asking fir trouble. We mak oor offerings as it bodes us weel."

This wasn't much to go on, apart from misbegotten fears about rituals they don't understand and scare stories about undead hosts and questing beasts. Missing children, rot in the crop, a mysterious new stranger in the temple? Could it be a witch? Some kind of carrier of wasting spirits?

"Your Seanadh, where do you make your offerings?"

The man grunted and twisted his face in surprise, one of his companions turned and almost spat his words across the table.

"Whit business is it o' yours, witch? An' you here on behalf o' the Order, an' aw? Come tae dig oot petty heracies an' prey upon good men and add the Order's chains tae oor hurt?"

"Shut it!" The foreman's hand slammed down loud enough that people across the tavern jumped in their seats, the clap leaving a silence hanging as the two men glared at one another barely a foot apart.

"Your Seanadh, where is it?"

He grumbled as he turned back to her, the mutterings on other tables returning, "the auld wood, whit's left o' it. The Order cut a path through tae their citadel but there's still a pairt fir the auld gods deep within it, far frae the pilgrimage road. But we paid oor dues, we gave whit's been asked o' us even efter the Order's temple wis built. That's oor way. We paid oor way."

Maybe they did. But for this village, at least, it seems additional payment has been claimed.

He continued, mumbling down into the tankard clasped in both hands, "ma grandfaither used tae say that the payment wis fir oor patron. The fox o' the willows, he ca'd it. It kept a watch ower us an' in return, we kept its willows. Long gone noo, those trees. Fell alang wi' the orchard wi' the path frae the sooth."

The Order and the road had been here for years. Why would the keepers of the wood abandon this township to such an intrusion by child-snatching creatures now?

He didn't leave her to her thoughts for long, looking up and meeting her eyes directly for the first time, "whit's yer name, Craw?" He said, leaning in a little. "No that Ah'd miss yon eyes o' yours if ye returned. Ye'll be back, right? Before the coming o' the Seanadh?"

She was careful not to let the question rest as her eyes rested on the coin she couldn't see but knew was clasped in his hands.

"My name is Fiadh, where is your township?"

"It's the Three Willows, mebbe a nicht's ride tae the north if ye came bi saddle." He paused for a moment, looking at her more intently than before, "Dae they aw look like ye, Fiadh? Aw the Craws? Dae they aw huv yon silvered eyes?"

She stood then, turning from his gaze, "they do, Oeric.

Don't spend that coin, I'll return for it when the deed is done."

***

The stonework was finely crafted, even beautiful in its own way. Kneeling figures carved in solemn rows gazed adoringly at the figure at the head of the archway.

Or, at least, where the figure should have stood. The keystone of the arch had been ripped free, torn through the shattered remnants of the door below it. She could still pick out the pieces, arms raised aloft here, sunbeams radiating outwards there.

No mere farmhand nor priest is strong enough for such destruction. Even if the men of the willows are the superstitious kind to take their anger out on stone. "Still boarded up", they had claimed back in the tavern. Whatever had torn its way through had done so long after the villagers had departed. Alone, in this still village only strange in its emptiness and silence under the cutting wind, this temple had been disturbed.

The grass around the entrance had been tended meticulously as if every blade had been trimmed to the perfect length to flatter the temple that stood among it. The bushes were the same, kept shapely in a way that seemed almost vain for such a structure.

She stepped across the boundary, flinching as she always did to enter the hallowed places of another, and cast her gaze about the shadowed hall.

The arched interior was held aloft by wooden pillars, small, like the township that it had served. Its roof was timber, not thatch, and supported by walls of stone. The faithful had worked hard to build this place, an effort that had not prevented whatever creature had smashed aside the benches in its entrance.

The wooden benches had been scattered, the hall itself a mess of shattered woodwork, splinters and spans littered and

11

piled high against the walls. She had seen this kind of destruction before, in too many places. Places of faith dashed by the fury of those who took insult at the proud symbols at their door or, as so often the case in this borderland between the old and the new, had themselves been laid low and driven out by the very people who erected these stones.

Her home had been one of these places, once.

She could smell it, too, now, snapping her from her reflections. Not the stench of some beast, but the unmistakable sickening sweetness of the recently deceased. She turned with care to look upon what she knew to already be there.

The corpse sat at the altar, still propped up in the ornate seat behind it, overshadowed by the great forked beams of the Lord's symbol. The light of the hall's sole opening into the sky lit him in a ghostly pale glow, as well as the gleam of a knife thrust through his hand into the resin-varnished altar below, still gripping a roll of parchment .

She could feel the blade at her back grow chill, as if the dead priest caused it to draw the scant heat from the air around them. Long silent, Caerdrich sensed something here and she had learned to keep their council. Such warnings from the sword had led her to escape from more than one monster in the dark.

Fiadh's eyes narrowed against the bright contrast of the hall as she stepped lightly towards the altar. She raised a sleeve across her face as she stepped up to the level of the altar and closer to the slowly deteriorating body who sat against it.

Caerdrich did not speak false, they never did. This priest was far too pale for even a man killed after weeks shut away in this hall.

He was ghostly pale. No veins protruded from the wrists that extended beneath decorated red robes of the priesthood of Alwealda, the God of those farmhands in the tavern and the southern kingdoms. His head lolled back, exposing a neck that had been torn at like the bite of a dog or…

Baobhan sith, perhaps? She had one answer to this mystery. Perhaps it was her kin who took this man, fed upon him, seduced him, and made him their puppet. The men of the village had run from it, leaving it to take their young. Perhaps they believed their coin could relieve their guilt.

It was a tempting theory but a false one. They had indeed abandoned this place, but not in a wild escape from any kind of fearsome beast. It was of no interest to farmers to lead a Crow into a trap, nor to hide from her the tell-tale signs of a bloodthirsty fey preying upon a township.

Nor would such a creature leave the corpse of its prey so... peaceful, its hand pinned against parchment. They cared nothing for identification when they were done feeding, nor would they celebrate their success with such wrathful destruction of a temple that held no meaning to them on their departure.

Something more was going on here, something Caerdrich could see but she could not, yet.

The knife had pierced the hand but there was no blood upon the altar, the priest had been drained of his blood before the blade had struck. Why? What possible purpose could it hold? What possible object of rage did he cling to?

Her hands moved with the utmost care, holding his grip in place as she drew the blade free, slowly, deliberately to avoid doing damage to the roll between his fingers.

The fingers prised apart, she opened the roll to something she had not expected. A mess of lines scrawled back and forth across the paper, less a careful last message and more the scrambled thoughts of a broken mind. The last lines were in an unintelligible hand, devolving into a black line stabbed across the page.

*The Lord claims his due, and I have given it. I have given every breath to his mission in this forsaken place.*

*He speaks to me in a different voice now, from beyond the veil. He guides me with a new purpose so I might give myself fully to his mission here. It may stain me, it may tarnish my name in the annals that will tell of this time, but it is in his name and his alone that I must work.*

*His whispers once came from beyond the veil but they guide my every step, now. They come to me in my dreams and from the shadows around me.*

*He whispers, and I listen.*

That last line sent a chill down her spine. She had heard people speak like that before. Not in a temple like this, not among the people of the south, but even in a different tongue the meaning was the same.

Whispers in the dark.

The whispering god had spoken to him, she could feel it, the sharp taste of his words still lingered in the air. This priest had been led astray, a man who had wandered from the path and been called to another by kind words and promises.

Lot had taken his soul long before another took his life.

But she was not here for a lost man's soul.

Fiadh ran her eyes across the altar, turning the sheets over one by one, looking for anything that might leave hints as to the nature of the creature who had come to this town and tore it from its normality--anything that was written in her tongue or that of the villagers of the Three Willows, not the opaque religious script of the Àrdish. A note by the priest to his order, perhaps. Notes to himself about his companions, or even better, discussing the children who had vanished under his eye.

The symbol of the Order was everywhere, the Lord's symbol encircled in the crimson wax of their seal. There was another scrawled into the corners of the paper, however. A variant, the circle instead crowned in the forked symbol in the shape of a two-headed key.

The whispers did not come at random. She had heard them herself, once. In a hall not dissimilar to this, a hallowed place of stone soon to be drawn to destruction by Lot's tempting words.

Caerdrich had sensed it. There was more to this place than simply another temple built on the ruins of a people long departed.

She began scanning the floor around her feet, crouching close to it, hand brushing back and forth just above the surface, frantic now. This was no longer about the coin of a village foreman.

There! Marks of the creature's footfall. But there was no sign of the long print of a woman, instead only the circular marks of something entirely different.

"Pawprints", she said, her eyes following the steps up and away from the altar. "In dust?" This holy man must have been at his seat for a long while before the creature killed him. Perhaps long enough that he was here when the townsfolk came knocking at his door, and yet he did not answer.

So, it was not one of the blood-drinkers after all. She might escape the stain of association to the death of another man of faith yet.

She grimaced at the thought. Too many saw the baobhan sith, with their rumoured power to take raven forms, and the Crows as two sides of the same coin. Where deaths came at the hand of the blood-drinkers then violence against those Crows who remained surely followed.

The prints ran away from the altar and they ran with a scattering of crimson drops, whether from the priest or the fey creature it was hard to tell. Fiadh followed them away and down, towards the corner of the room and a smear running across the wall and floor.

What has been done here? Had the priest become the unwitting servant of a demon in his own temple? Deceived by the whispers as to its true nature?

She followed the prints in the dust, clear circles in the dust. But when they came to the rear of the temple, they were different. No longer a line of pawprints in the dust, but a swathe of prints and scuffs. All before a back-door closed flush against the timber walls, lined in iron trim and crisscrossed with further support in the grey metal.

"The children's feet. They were alive," she said, whispered

words lost into the howls of wind beyond the walls.

Fiadh sighed and sat back on her heels. It was one thing to go back to the inn with news that whatever creature that had plagued the town was gone together with their mislead priest, quite another to come with the news that so were their children. They've lost so much already. Should they return here they might walk straight back into the embrace of the whispers which had already led one more prepared than they astray.

Selfishly, there was also unlikely to be any thanks for the messenger of that news. Including the reward promised for ridding this town of its rot.

But Caerdrich's chill pricked at the hairs on the back of her neck. It was a warning, she knew. There was yet more to this place, somewhere.

"What can you see, blade?" She said, her gaze running over every feature of the temple around her, searching for anything that might reveal a deeper truth.

Fiadh crouched and brushed at the slats of wood forming the floor, following the edges of the scuffs and trails of crimson. There was a split here, where the slats had been cut short in a neat line. There was a section that had been splintered, too, fragments of rusty nails remained where something had been torn free. A handle, and a handle meant that this had been meant to be lifted.

Following the dead at the beckoning of a sword was not the intended ending of a small job to banish some imagined monster from a temple. But her task here was not yet done.

Her fingers failed to find purchase on the edges of the split boards. They were finely crafted, clearly the product of a great deal of investment by the local townsfolk. This may have been a longhouse once, the hall of some small Laird or shrine to the old gods before the Order travelled north into their lands.

There was no purchase possible without a handle. This was no task for sgeanan or sword. Unfortunately, this obstacle could not be tackled with subtlety.

Fiadh stood and released her cloak, placing it carefully to one side as she glanced about the hall. Something heavy, with weight and leverage, a stand perhaps or… there! A tall metal candle stand was leaning against the pews. Of northern make, it seemed unusual for a place of prayer but there were few who could match the handiwork of the Sjøfolk with iron. It would be a shame to damage such ornate handiwork for such a menial task but needs must.

Her woollen surcoat and braces of blades followed folded over her cloak, leaving bare arms free for the task at hand. The scabbard holding Caerdrich was shifted to remain hung over her shoulder away from her waist where it might hamper her swing. The cold air of the hall pricked at her skin, and she felt a shiver run across her shoulders. No matter, it would soon be a welcome relief.

The base of the stand struck home to splinters but little more. It rose and fell as Fiadh fell into a rhythm, bringing it overhead in a long sweep to her right, left hand gripping fast at the base of the candle's holder. The wood shuddered, then cracked, each blow tearing further into the beams. One beam began to break away, then another, breaking off and tumbling down into the void beneath. As the third snapped and fell she halted the swings, placing the battered and dented stand to one side.

Her breaths came heavy, their misty clouds swept up with the steam rising from her shoulders. The sweat already ran cold against her skin, the first chills of the coming winter clinging to her close and stripping away the heat of her labour.

Crouching once more she gripped the edge of her new opening in the floor and pulled hard. It came up easily enough, a door half as tall as a man rising up on quiet hinges and falling back along the rear wall. Below her, now, a series of stone steps far older than the woodwork around it stretched down to a paved floor below.

Fiadh sighed, swinging Caerdrich's scabbard from her shoulder and into her hands. Nothing good ever came from underground, there was nothing worth hiding from view beneath the earth that wasn't hidden because that was where it could not do harm.

The air drifting from the opening was stale, carrying nothing more strongly than moisture and rot. Rot with the distinct tang of iron.

She took the first steps carefully, the soft steps of her boots drowned out by the wind's howl about the walls. Her left hand wrapped about Caerdrich's hilt, a momentary shift in grip giving her the comfort of the easy movement of the well-oiled blade.

Nothing greeted her steps, and there was little of note in the dank corridor that ran below the rear of the temple. The rough stone of the steps was matched by its walls and the paved floor beneath, protrusions of moss and weed clearly left untended for months, if not years.

Two doors were embedded in the wall running beneath the main hall of the temple, near-identical slabs of roughly hewn wood held in place by cords of iron crisscrossing their fronts in a mirror of the one above them. Twin bolts ran their width, but both lay unsealed. One had been firmly hauled closed, the other hung open.

From that doorway ran the streak of blood that stained the temple above.

It was quieter beneath the floor, the shriek of the wind dampened by the descent. The quiet was unnerving, it always was in places that should be walked by so many, but it gave some comfort that there would not be any beast or man waiting to respond to her unwelcome intrusion.

Still, feet rolling softly into each step, Fiadh progressed following the trail of blood with her hand still wrapped firmly around Caerdrich's leather.

The room beyond the doorway was wreathed in darkness, no windows reaching up to cast light on the bare stonework ground. She squinted as she slid sideways through the opening, careful not to disturb the door or brush against its frame.

Within Fiadh could make out a line of cots framing the room, simple wooden frames holding hay mattresses above the floor.

There was, lying sprawled on that floor at the foot of one of these cots, a child. Lifeless, drained, limp. The blood ran from them across the centre of the room and through the doorway in which she stood. Just one left to hint at the fate of the others who had disappeared from this village over the past months.

A confirmation of the fate a part of her knew had already fallen upon them. But still, faced with confirmation of her fears, she knew this was not everything. Caerdrich did not stir to something as banal as death. Something lay deeper still within the horrors of this place she had yet to uncover. Even with their silence the blade remained a useful companion.

She saw the child clearer now as she crossed the threshold, saw the rugged gash running about the child's throat mirroring that of the priest slumped at the altar above. But, as Fiadh knelt at their side, she could see the wound was not of the same kind. It was sharp and deep, made by blade rather than bite.

Caerdrich had guided her well. There was more to this than the feeding ground of a twisted fey.

Her eyes could not help but run up to the child's face. Eyes still wide, frozen in fear, fixed on a distance seeking aid that would never come. Or, at least, could not come soon enough.

She couldn't shake her gaze from them. Her heart felt like it had fallen through a hole in her gut, and the cold cut close. Everything else seemed to fade away around those sightless, haunted eyes.

The scuff of her boot on stone startled her, breaking a silence she had not realised had fallen so completely. There was no sound of wind here, no creaking of the timbers of the temple above.

She walked to the wall and ran a hand along the joint between the stonework and the wood above. Frowning,

Fiadh gave it a knock. There was no response, no hollow thunk of knuckles on floorboards.

Continuing along its surface more knocks returned more solid taps. This floor was more than just a floor. It was packed with soil.

This space was designed not to let a single sound journey into the temple above. It wasn't the work of any witch or spirit. Those who erected the temple above had sealed this space, and it was in the silence below the earth that the children had been hidden.

So, who had let them out?

Above each of the cots hung chains, each a single hook holding bands of iron.

Cold iron. Like the doorway to this chamber, like the one at the rear of the temple above.

Fiadh's search took her back to the doorway, running her free hand across the surface. Her silver eyes pierced the darkness and saw the gleam of grey metal running across its surface, the bolt that enabled the room to be sealed from the outside alone.

The metal was darkened in places as if scorched. In isolated spots at first as if a flame had been put against it gingerly, careful to avoid touching the wood beneath. Then there was a wide expanse of the burn, a hand's width across, marked in raised bumps of ash.

It was as if someone had rubbed a lit torch against the bar, creating a layer of ash across the iron that might shield its surface.

She moved back into the corridor and across to the other door. There were no such marks here. The locking bar had been returned with quite some difficulty, clumsily, panicked. The scuffs against the frame betrayed that it had been sealed by someone unused to handling the mechanism.

Fiadh loosened the belt about her waist and pulled it free, wrapping it about her free hand with several twists. There was no telling what had burned the surface of the iron, and her years on the road had taught her that such precautions were a wise step to avoiding inviting the same pain on herself.

Belt tight around her hand she grasped the locking mechanism and pulled.

The stench that rose to meet her was fouler still than she had expected, and her arm instinctively came to cover her face as the door cracked open just a sliver.

There was more here, though. The hairs on her skin stood on end, chills running from her fingertips to her skull. It lingered, something deeper than the smell, a rot that ran into the very stone at her feet. It flowed freely through the space and it was all she could bear to stand still for a moment and not bolt back up the steps.

Fiadh's eyes shone, their silver peering into the gloom that ran free of the crack. It glowed with spite and radiated cruelty. Waves of revulsion flowed through her; no human should stand on such a threshold.

It was why they offered a Crow gold to stand here instead.

Her knuckles were white between the straps of the belt as she gripped the hilt of Caerdrich tight, one foot reaching out and pushing the door open.

The room was smaller than the previous one but no less shrouded in shadow and oppressive silence. Fiadh could spy a series of candle stands against the walls and a desk which had once held the papers now scattered across the room.

They lay scattered across a dark stain on the ground just beyond her feet, a wide circle containing another and yet another within it. Within each circle were scrawled symbols in the same darkness, but where it came to her feet the circles were broken, scuffed, smeared across the paved floor.

But the patterns didn't hold her gaze, for there was something far darker beyond them. The gloom that only her silvered eyes could discern from the shadows was spilling from an object framed against the far end of the room. A bronze apparatus had been erected and secured against the floor and ceiling; a frame as large as a man. Hanging from it was a tattered shroud of translucent cloth, shifting in a breeze she could not feel.

From behind it, the gloom fell, spilling over every surface, caressing every sheet and object as it poured through the door and into the corridor behind her.

Fiadh's mind raced. What nature of place was this? What lay beyond the shroud that would drench this place in such darkness? What did the symbols mean?

She needed to know what this was, close it before it could poison not just this temple but the village beyond.

She moved as fast and efficiently as she could, her heart raising and cold sweat breaking out across her brow. She swept up papers from across the floor in turn, desperately running her eyes across them. They were a mix of different scrawls, from the polished and delicate to frantic scratches.

They were in different hands, some crumpled and faded as if stuffed away to be brought here. This was not the work of a single man but many.

All writing in a text she could not read.

Fiadh swore as she continued to flip over page after page, looking for anything written in a language she could understand. There was none. The letters were as she'd expected, some of the words seemed as if they should be Àrdish but twisted and ornate, some kind of archaic language shared by the priest and his colleagues.

All of it.

Enough with the words, then, she flipped back through looking for pictures or diagrams that would give her some clue of their purpose. There were some, mostly collections of symbols and geometric shapes that resembled the scrawling on the floor, though she could not tell if their purpose was for measurements or some ritualistic procedure.

But there was one thing that stood out. A collection of papers tattered and darkened by age which displayed an ornate orb, illustrated in detail and from different perspectives, arrows and script indicating where it had been altered and moved from position to position.

Why hold such instruction without an object to carry it out on?

Fiadh dropped the papers and began to move across the room methodically, eyes piecing the dark, scanning the floor for such an object.

There it was, back up against one of the corners of the room, a small metal orb the size of a fist.

It glinted in what little light there was, highlighting the intricate carvings across its surface. No, not carvings, each curve of metal was a separate piece interlocked into the device.

One piece shifted under her palm and Fiadh hissed as it caught on skin and a droplet of blood ran into its cracks.

She cast her eyes about, at the indecipherable pages on the desk, the blood of children gone staining the engraved floor, and that veil hanging before the darkness that poured forth like smoke.

She was done with shouldering this mystery in silence. She swore, feeling the heat rising in her, the hot rage of the injustice that had occurred here.

"Caerdrich, what fey is there that could operate such a device?"

She knew the answer, but she had asked anyway. An extra moment of seeding doubt she no longer held. It was no fey who had used this space, who had stolen the children of the Three Willows, who had trapped them down here in the dark and cut them open one by one in a ritual designed by those who had never stepped foot on this ground.

Fiadh turned once more to the veil, that infernal contraption that held it aloft, whose design had cost this village so much to grant it nothing but loss.

The blade's chill became a harsh cold, the very air around them seeming to frost and the bite turning her hand white. Caerdrich beckoned her beyond the veil, in pursuit of the darkness.

What could lay beyond it? The souls of those lost? The children who had disappeared from these chambers, sent on as sacrifice to whatever fearsome god this dead priest had shut himself away to serve?

Her eyes fell to the orb again, cast down, her mind drifted back to the burns across the iron brackets at the door, at the single body left in the adjoining room.

"He never opened it."

The realisation came to her suddenly. He had shut himself away despite being sent here to serve the village, along with the creature who had previously been seen free at his side. A fey that would burn at the touch of cold iron.

"He never could, he couldn't work out the key to pass beyond the veil. All his efforts came to nothing. That's why he reached out, that's why he…"

… listened to the whispers that came in the night.

She turned to the doorway behind her once again. That's why he died. Killed to free the children that remained. Murdered on the cusp of his completion of whatever ritual he was guided by the whisperer beyond the veil.

She thought back, to the doorway torn down at the front of the temple. No fey who chose to kill by bite achieved that. Something else was brought here after the death of the priest.

Something capable of taking the children away. To a place beyond whether neither the priest nor the villagers could find them. On the very eve of the Seanadh.

Fiadh remembered the farmer's words, there was a place they knew from before. The woods with a place for the old gods deep within it.

It was time to leave this dark place. Caerdrich would know the path. The blade had survived generations passed hand to hand in these very woods and hills. They would lead her where she had to go.

But what of the fate of this place? What if the misguided and lost returned to hear the whispers, to follow their guidance to tear aside the veil  and attempt a journey to what lies beyond once again? How many more dead eyes would gaze up from these halls, their futures snatched away by the greed of those chasing knowledge that would cost more than they had any right to offer?

Fiadh spat her response to the darkness from behind a

snarl. There will be no one to return to this place, she would leave them no place for them to return to.

"I'll burn it to the ground and let the gods fight over the ashes."

\*\*\*

Dìleas bore her through the trees as fast as he was able, the branches tearing at her hair and leathers, crashing between fir and birch, his hooves dancing across earth and roots.

Fiadh's knuckles were white on her pommel, her heels held tight against Dìleas' haunches. She could feel the dawn rising behind her, the sun's light racing her to the heights. Even now its glow would be lighting the peaks, running down their sides, spilling towards their goal.

If the light reached them before she did they would be gone, spirited away from her grasp, never again to rejoin their families.

They would not be the first to be lost, nor the last. But this time she could not, would not, let this chance get away.

They were not alone among these ancient woods. Howls and barks like a hundred hounds rung between the pines.

They may have left the village to its fate, but the old guardian had not abandoned the trees and the altar that lay beyond them.

"Where? Guide me, blade."

She felt Caerdrich's presence, the pressure at the edges of her mind that pulled and pushed so that she might follow the long-lost path.

The trees were pressing close and Fiadh's vision swam as the light was driven out by the grasping branches. Their trunks hemmed close, forcing Dìleas to swerve from side to side to evade them. Carved faces gazed back at her from them, emotionless eyes beneath great antlers whipped by.

The face of Cernos lived in this shade, it was the spirit of Cernos that pursued her, baying and barking in the dawn's light.

But they were rising, every bound of Dileas bearing them higher away from the forest floor and towards their destination. The sound of the beast of the woods fell away behind them as the warm glow of dawn began to break through the canopy and light their path. Ahead roots made way to rock, and the dirt was replaced with stone steps placed upon the side of the ascent.

The steps were overgrown and broken but her steed was no beast of burden or wagon horse accustomed to the paved tracks of the lowlands. He picked his way higher swiftly and with the confidence of the shaggy breeds that were bred among the peaks and hills of Seann Àite.

Finally, they were free, the branches making way to clear skies and the steps to a wide-open space where the stone had long ago surrendered to the grasses and weeds that had reclaimed this hilltop.

Fiadh dismounted and gave Dileas' sweat-drenched haunches a pat as she stepped towards the centre of this ancient stone circle. Old cairn stones had tumbled and cracked; furrows carved into the stone floor now overtaken by lichen. They shone with dull light as her eyes passed over them, far fainter than the runes that had graced the circles of home. It had been many years since the people of Three Willows had truly tended to this place with the respect it was due.

The altar, which once must have been the pride of the community that had called this region home, had been split into two crumbling chunks. On one half, seemingly the only structure still standing upright where it was intended to be, sat clay bowls and plates long devoid of any contents. The remnants of a past Seanadh, perhaps.

Beyond it was what she was seeking. Rising ahead was the síd, a great mount of earth punctured by a yawning mouth held open by slabs of flagstone. As the sun passed the horizon it could well be an opening to the realm of the daoine sìth. For now, exactly the kind of place you might use to shelter those unable to build shelter for themselves.

Fiadh stepped cautiously forward, Caerdrich's scabbard once more in one hand, her other on its hilt. The dawn's light had not yet reached the mouth, cloaking it in shadow that her eyes could not adjust to whilst out in the open.

But she could hear them, the scuffs of leather on the rock, the whispers of children who had been beckoned to stay quiet but couldn't quite grasp it, the hushes of their elders who had heard the arrival of hooves outside.

She gave Dileas a rap on the rump, letting him wander on and off the flat and back into the trees in search for something to graze upon and crouched low, waiting for any response from the shadows. Nothing, yet. More whispers as they heard the horse move away but nothing more, not even the barks of the guardian she had left behind in the woods.

Then there was movement, one figure venturing out into the light, one hand held over their head to shade their eyes from the rising sun. She froze, eyes fixed on Fiadh's crouched form with one hand on Caerdrich's scabbard and the other outstretched for balance.

Slowly, with her free hand raised and palm open, Fiadh fought against the chill that ran up her arm from the blade and placed the scabbard on the ground, the frost dancing across the stones and dew across the grass freezing upon their stems.

The blade's anger bit at her fingers but now was not the time to placate them, she had the feelings of others to sooth first.

Her jaw clenched with the effort of holding a smile even as the cold gripped at her hand and stabbed up her arm. Still the girl stood frozen, eyes wide and darting between Fiadh and the darkness of the opening behind her.

"Still, child, I'm not here to hurt you," Fiadh said in the softest tone she could conjure. She took a step forward, hand still held up and open. "I've seen the temple, I promise you will never have to go back to that place again, I'm here to return you to your parents."

She took another step and the girl stiffened and ran back into the dark. Fiadh swore, wondering how she could have better worded her intent. Too late now.

She straightened and with a lingering glance at the blade lying flat among the dead vegetation about it, headed towards the opening.

Within was a chamber far smaller than the gaping entrance suggested might lie beyond. A single space with what may once have been a stone table in its centre, now little more than a mound protruding from the rough-hewn rock.

In the corner, cowering in a huddle with the girl who had ventured to the entrance attempting to shield them all with nothing but her outstretched arms, were a dozen children curled in sudden silence.

She crouched, sitting back on her heels, and tried desperately to bring a genuine smile to her face. This wasn't her speciality, but children seemed to like adults who were at their own level rather than looming over them. Right now, though, it didn't seem to be calming their fears.

There had to be something else she could do, surely? How had she felt those many years ago when her own home was taken from her, when she had heard the whispers and witnessed the intent of men long led astray?

Hungry, that was one feeling she could remember with complete clarity. Fiadh pulled her pack down from her shoulders and, with a moment to rummage, came across some scraps of two-day-old bread, salted meat, and a pair of apples.

It was meagre fair but with some luck she'd be dining out on the coin of their parents for some time after today. She pulled it free in the loose cloth that wrapped them and tossed the collection in the direction of the children.

The eldest of them barely moved, their eyes fixed on her, but the younger ones' attention was drawn immediately to the apple that rolled free and across the stones.

Not enough, yet, but their trust would be hard to earn. It had been shattered by someone far closer to them than a strange warrior from a far place, dressed all in black.

The apple came to rest in a groove and Fiadh saw it lit from beneath, more symbols carved into the floor as outside. Here, though, she knew them well. Without the weather to soften them and vegetation to crack them time had not broken this script. Her fingers traced the edges of it, reading the words.

*Whenever the night is darkest,*
*However long the winter might draw on,*
*Fear not, children of the woods,*
*For the sun will always rise again.*

There was no need to read the words once more, to search for meaning in foreign script here. This was her tongue, the language of the folk who had once called the Three Willows home, the words of these rolling hills and deep forests.

In years gone by they marked this place as a home and shelter against the encroaching cold. They had lived here, and at dawn and dusk brought gifts in thanks to the lord of the woods who kept watch over them until they departed.

This place was once the hearth of a god long passed into mist. But another had returned to tend to the village of Three Willows, one who for generations kept watch over their children until they were snatched away. Fiadh's eyes followed the script as it ran about the stone mound and out towards the entrance.

Another who comes in the form of a fox, perhaps?

It stood at the mouth of the cave with golden eyes fixed upon her, its shadow cast far by the light of a brightening sky now spilling through its entrance. The fox of the willows had come back for the children of the village, even when their own families had fled.

Its gaze lingered for a moment longer before turning away and padding away in a wide circle clear of the black scabbard that still lay in the centre of the stone circle.

Fiadh turned back for a moment, hesitating as she found

the eyes of the children still set upon her. They did not trust her, she would not, in their place. But they may trust the fox, who had delivered them to this place from the horrors that lay below the now smouldering ruins of the village temple.

Perhaps if she could win its trust, she could win theirs.

As Fiadh stood and walked back towards the entrance she saw that the fox was not alone. It had walked to the far side, where the cairns had tumbled into the trees, and it walked into the shadow of a far greater and stranger creature.

The beast stood as tall as Dileas, but it was no beast of burden. Slit eyes peered at her from the face of a snake, its serpentine neck fading into the mottled coat stretched thin over the lithe and muscle-bound body of a predator. The split hooves of a deer pawed at the stone, but the low chorus of warning that emerged from its throat as she entered the sunlight reminded her that those feet would rather trample her than bear it in flight.

Those hundred howls had never come not from a pack, but from one creature alone. The guardian of the woods, this questing beast, the spirit of Cernos.

At its side, the fox turned and hesitated but a moment before it rose onto its hind legs and began to shed its animal form. From the shadow rose a woman, but not a woman that would mingle among humanity without disguise. Fur still clung to her hips and it was the clawed pads of a fox that graced this hallowed ground.

Pads that had graced not just this place, but the halls of a temple before it.

The eyes flickered the gold of the fox before fading to a ruddy brown. This, then, had been the companion of the priest who the villagers had so distrusted. The very same being who they had offered gifts to for the Seanadh, whose entrapment by that priest had surrendered their fields to rot.

With her hands turned towards Fiadh she could see the black and blistered skin of her palms. The burn of cold iron against fey flesh. The burns of having pulled free a single bar from a single door to free the children who had been locked within.

Fiadh was kneeling, now, though she couldn't remember when she had chosen to do so. It was to her bowed head the fey spoke.

"Welcome, Crow, we were not sure that you would come."

The sound of cànan, her own tongue, was like a song after so long conversing in Àrdish.

"But for what purpose?" she continued. "You have already set fire to the evidence of wrongdoing in the Three Willows. The rot came for their crops, the woods came for their children, now a Crow came for their temple. Yet you come here and despoil this ground with your accursed blade. For what purpose?"

The beast chattered, the breaths of many creatures mingling in a staccato growl as Fiadh's eyes glanced across at the black scabbard.

"We have an arrangement, the blade and I," she said, not raising her gaze from it.

"No good will come of it," responded the fox.

"It is not good that we seek together, but I shall try and do some good along the road."

"We cannot simply let this transgression pass. Others displaced those who we watched over, but none have been so bold as to bring such a blade onto this ground. None have been, so none shall be. Do you challenge us, Crow?"

Fiadh kept her eyes cast down, her hands relaxed. Alone she could not challenge the guardian, but the blade could, should she move fast enough to reach it. But the beast was faster than she, and who could tell what wrath Cernos might bring down on those who would spill the blood of his own at the foot of his hearth?

"It need not come to that," she said, as softly and steadily as she could manage. "I might die, but so might you, and leave this place to fall to those who would destroy it and raise it anew in their own image."

There was silence, for a moment. The fey tended not to

respond as humans would, their thought impassive and opaque, and they had no reason to pander to human expectations on their own ground.

"We cannot simply let them return, you know that, Crow. We have seen what fellow men will do to them. We have seen the cruelty, the selfish designs of those who would use their suffering to serve their own ends. We cannot simply stand by and risk those we have taken into our care."

"See it in their eyes," the fox continued. "See the pain and consider what you ask of us."

Fiadh turned her head to see that the children had come to the mouth of the cave behind her, gathered in a huddle supporting one another, the eldest still standing at the front and shielding the youngest.

But that wasn't all her eyes saw. One of the foremost of them, a girl who stood to the front with all the confidence of age but the stature of one barely a dozen winters in age, looked back at her with eyes that did not fully reflect the dark rings of the others.

There were flecks of silver in those eyes. Silver that would set a child to age far slower than those around her, silver that would one day overtake her irises and grant her the gift to look deep into the darkest of places.

Eyes Fiadh shared.

*They are only children*, she thought.

*So was I*, came the response from the back of her mind.

*It wasn't the same, was it?*

She stood and walked back to the group. They shrunk back from her, all apart from the two eldest and this one exceptional child whose chin was raised high in defiance.

Fiadh knelt before the girl, placing a hand on each of her shoulders, "what's your name, girl?"

"It's..." the girl hesitated, her eyes searching Fiadh's own for her intent. "It's Orlaith."

"Who is your mother, Orlaith?"

She shook her head sharply. There was no mother waiting in the town for a lost daughter with silvered eyes, there never was. The Àrdish have few ways of treating a suspected changeling, of which abandonment was a fate gentler than the others. Whether living or dead it wouldn't be long before a girl like Orlaith was stolen away by another like the dead priest in a ruined temple.

She looked into Orlaith's eyes, there was fear there, of course there was, but there was grit there as well. She could thrive here, perhaps, as many might not. It was that or be abandoned once more to the violence of frightened men.

It was settled, then. If the fey needed to have saved something from a village plagued by the rot of crops and whispers, then they could save one. One who had already been abandoned by the people who had denied her a true place to call home already.

She stood slowly and turned to face the pair, "Orlaith will stay among your kind, you may raise her as your own, as past children of the forest have been raised. But the others will return to their homes. With their own kind where they belong."

The silence followed once more as the fox fixed her with those deceptively brown eyes. The beast circled her once, pausing for but a moment before loping into the trees beyond.

"You have made a proposal we can accept, Crow. We shall protect her as we have done all before her. But the Three Willows will not thrive if they cannot make peace with the ruin they have wrought upon themselves."

Fiadh walked over to her black scabbard, aware of the eyes on her but moving with all the certainty she could muster.

"Their pact is not mine to give", she said, her hand folding over the icy leather and passing its belt over her shoulder. "I cannot grant it. But I can promise you that I will return those you release into my care safely."

She turned towards the fox, now standing alone between the toppled cairns. "I have only one question of you before we depart."

The fey nodded her acceptance.

"What was behind the veil in the temple, in the room of the seal you broke to permit the guardian of these woods to tear open the way for you to depart?"

The eyes of the fey fixed her with a stare fiercer than before, the stillness of her face breaking only for a moment as the muscles tensed in her cheeks.

"Nothing," the fox said, her hand waving away the question. "A curtain on a wall, that was all. The focus of so much suffering was just the obsessions of a broken mind."

They raised a hand dismissively, as if the happenings below the temple were only so much of a nuisance.

"Depart, Crow, before the sun opens the way to An Síth and we change our minds."

Fiadh did not push further. With a whistle she heard the hooves of Dìleas bearing him up from the trees and she turned to her new charges. It would be a long morning's travel back to the tavern on the beaten path, but at least it would be the last walk of this wretched journey.

***

The once-lonely tavern was now bustling. News travelled fast, and families who had fled to Dun Caraich had flocked back to the roadside where the children of the Three Willows waited for them.

There were tearful reunions. Adults threw their arms around their children, searching their eyes for the harm they knew had befallen them. More there, besides. They had been returned from the fey and no true Àrdish would accept such a gift without checking that they had not been duped by a child with the form of their offspring but the eyes of another.

But there were also adults searching over and over again through the children who remained in increasing panic. They would not find who they were looking for.

Too many of them wouldn't.

Fiadh stood leaning against Dìleas at some distance. She knew how this worked. No one wanted to be faced with the reminder that it was an outsider who needed to be brought in to save their own when they could not.

In time, though, the foreman she had spoken to only yesterday would drag himself from the others and slump in her direction.

He would not meet her eyes, nor entirely face her as he rummaged deep into a satchel and pulled free a purse ringing with the metal held within. His gaze continued to glance up at the horizon, where smoke still rose in a trail up from the village beyond.

"So, there wis a demon in that temple, then?" He muttered, looking deep into the purse as if he hadn't counted out its contents more than once already.

"That there was."

"A fat lot o' use the faith did him if it couldnae even keep a monster oot." He drew the purse strings tight and paused with a moment in his hand. He looked again out at the lingering smoke before holding it out in her direction, his gaze turning to the milling families down the road.

"That it didn't," she said.

Fiadh waited a moment before taking the purse. She considered making some joke, anything to break the tension. But she couldn't feel any of the warmth she'd drawn on teasing the man just yesterday. She had her coin. That would be enough. Now she could ride free of this place and hopefully put the eyes of the child below the temple far from her mind forevermore.

There was a break in the reunions on the road. Someone stamping back and forth, red robes of a layman of the order sweeping around, dragging in the mud. He stopped for a moment in the crowd before turning his head in toward them, eyes alight with rage. Storming in their direction he began jabbing a finger towards her.

"Whaur is she?" he snapped. "Whaur's Orlaith?"

Fiadh did not move from her relaxed lean against her saddle, but she noted the split wooden stave he gripped in one hand, its miniature hung about his neck, a mirror of

Oeric's own. She noted the haphazard stomp of his furious steps, and the manner in which his neck protruded forwards from slumped shoulders.

"Whaur is she, ye witch?" he said, waving a hand to quiet Oeric. "Whit huv ye done wi' her, whit accursed ritual did ye carry oot in yer bargains wi' the deevil?"

"Simon, she…" Oeric began, before the man's flailing hand again silenced him.

"Ye burned the laid's hoose! Ye took her frae me! Ye hud no richt! Witch! She wis mine by richt…" his words were cut off into a gurgle as Fiadh's fist struck his throat. He staggered back for barely a moment before the gurgle became a strangled yelp, collapsing to the ground as his knee gave way beneath Fiadh's foot.

"Whit huv ye done?" Oeric shouted, rushing to the side of the felled man. "Ye broke him, oor layman!" His stoic demeanour was broken, the stiff restraint he had displayed ever since they met falling away all at once.

Simon gurgled his complaint in response, stave lying abandoned, hands wrapped around an unnaturally twisted limb.

"I'll huv tae gie yin o' ma ain men in his place, I brocht ye here! Ye burned it aw an' noo ye strike him doon. It'll cost me a year's harvest, ye owe us…".

"I owe you nothing." Fiadh cut him off, packing the purse into her saddle bag and hauling herself onto Dìleas' back.

"You had a worm in your midst, Àrderman." she continued from above him. "A worm who spread rot through your people. If you wish to reclaim the Three Willows, you'd best leave him behind."

She looked down at the prostrate form of the layman with a snarl. "Let the wolves and ravens have him. They'll gain more from his bones than you ever did from his whispers."

Fiadh squeezed Dileas' flank and with a whistle he pulled away and down the track, leaving the barked complaints of Oeric behind her.

In the distance, she knew, a fox looked down on the

tavern and waited for those who might return to the willows and the smouldering remains of a dark past they might well put behind them.

That was a future she would have no part in, nor would she waste thoughts for a village that lost itself long ago.

Fiadh ran her hand down and into her saddlebag, running her fingers along the rough fibres of the grey veil sequestered there. The mystery of what lay beneath it called to her, a journey for another place, and another time.

# ABOUT THE AUTHOR

Tristan Gray was a latecomer to Scotland, moving to the north from Jersey in 2014.

After years of searching to find the real spark behind his writing Scotland unlocked it - The rugged country and dark history, which also inspired the works of George R. Martin and Diana Gabaldon, gave new meaning to the fantasy tales of his childhood.

Now, with a new connection to an adopted home driving his work, and inspiration stretching from conventional novels, to graphic novels, to games, Tristan is writing tales worthy of the inspiration by the land around him.

He can be found at his website:
tristangraywrites.com